ALEX EPICURE

THOUGHTS,
ON THE
ROAD

Laugh, cry, get angry

To Elizabeth
and Anthony
We work at a terrace.
a gived glance and I know,
we are spring out of
the same juice
whatever put is.

plul

THOUGHTS, ON THE ROAD

© 2022 ALEX EPICURE

SECOND EDITION, FIRST TRANSLATION

PRINT: AMAZON.COM

ISBN 9798832728926

COVER AND PHOTOS WERE PHOTOGRAPHER

ISN'T MENTIONED: ALEX EPICURE

GRAPHIC LAYOUT: ALEX EPICURE AND BEATRICE

ACKNOWLEDGEMENT TO ÅKE HÖGMAN FOR READING THROUGH

AND GIVING ME A WELL NEEDED THUMBS UP. THANK YOU!

To my newfound friend

Aphorisms, in any language, are built on mental structures, ideas, even ghosts, before any thoughts are spent on grammar. And if the writer grows together with his new language later in life, the original patterns of the mother tongue is more visible, if let to be.

This is a Swede writing in English, and not pretending to be anything else, absolutely not an English literature professor trying to eat of a smorgas bord. This is the whole idea with this little paperback. But being unique or impossible to understand is two very different things. I am very honoured that a newfound friend stepped in and diffused typos and linguistic flounders, making this little spur of wild thoughts a pleasant read. For me at least.

From my deepest, most watery blue
Thank you **Romas Tauras Viesulas**

Photo: Jorge Carcavelos

Preface

There has always been a desire for discovery within me, to live in new environments, to meet new people, and think new thoughts. It's an on-going, unquenchable thirst that governs my decisions, if I am allowed to make them myself. Sitting in a house and waiting for death does not suit me.

Leaving fixed points, seeking new horizons, is not a journey A to B, not even to Z. To be let into new worlds, one of the most important conditions is a mental attitude to dare to let go of the old. In the metamorphosis that you then go through, anything can happen, and the most amazing, frightening and uplifting thing is that repressed thoughts bubble to the surface. To enter new realms these thoughts have to be let out. I've done so, unfettered.

Many incoherent thoughts that came out of me during the journey of my first book didn't fit the context, but were still too good to be dismantled and scrapped back to dust. Here you have them in a book of their own, straight up, without shyness or censorship. Maybe liberating to read, maybe a start of something new.

I am here

I'm always here. But here is sometimes there, for you. I never get to there. I've tried. "I'm there!" I say, but it's a lie. The mind is where the leap is possible. But even my mind isn't there, it never seem able to stay, restlessly pushing another border. Worrying it would be trapped and killed if it didn't.

So it were when I left my homeland,
and didn't.

"The mental state of an ideal citizen…"

#babylon

A welded sculpture of old machine parts found somewhere around Sei-gnosse, France. It was my first longer stop on my escape from the "elongated country". Guess how I perceived the symbolism?

Waste for some, gold for others

A life well wasted. A perfect summation of how others look at freethinkers like me, and how I feel about my decisions in life. I've saved this old T-shirt just because of that. The material barely holds up, the print is as strong as ever.

#epicurism #gettingbackonmyfeet

Life : I

Without the ups and downs in life it would be flat-line, which is the equivalent of death.

Divorce it

Consumerism in a nutshell. More and better, never satisfied. Every dime spent edges away from happiness, with love as gift-wrapped emptiness.

A wall in the LX-factory, Lisbon. Formerly one of Lisbon's coolest neighborhoods in an old factory site, but now taken over by tourist consumerism… Still worth a visit

A prepositioned proposition

"Read my book at one of those squeezed out Lisbonian squares, where the loquat fruits are jealously yellow, and people breaths, calmly, as they talk, and curse for the fun of it."

To a friend going for a weekend in Lisbon, and promised to read a book of mine.

Forty-two

Today's rain provoked some thoughts about the strive for Artificial Intelligence.

Is it that we are so afraid of dealing with earth's huge environmental problems that we turn to an insentient computer? By accrediting it intelligence we expect it to solve our problems instead of doing anything about it ourselves. But as it's only a program programmed by humans it will never succeed in making anything else than 2+2=4, when we actually need it to say 42…

When I hear about a program that's made for playing chess but suddenly stops and instead produces the replacement for plastic, or invents renewable energy, then I believe in it. Until then, stop boasting about it.

#ai #notreally #standupanddosomething #rainbowwarriors

Ahead of future

Fossilization in the far future when humans have gone instinct. Really big Cockroaches dig in the sand and say, "Hmm, this is a typical human instrument from the neoplastic period. They apparently used it for ritual garments stored in small spaces. No one has ever figured out why they changed from better materials like wood. They where very short-sighted and finally finished off their own species."

Impressions found in the mud at Praia Almagraira,
Baleal, Portugal.

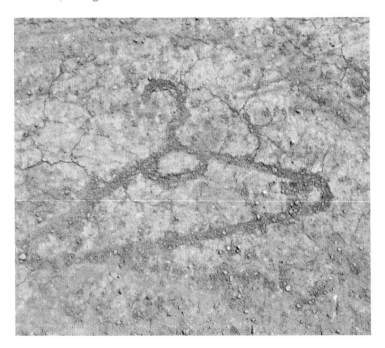

Te amo roca gris y antigua.
Te amo arbol tocado del viento.
Te amo grama resistente.
Te amo alma de todo, fuerza de cosmos y tierra,
historia y futuro, lo malo y lo bueno.
Me levantes con alegría y respeto.
Estoy volando caminando.
Montaña Durangoa,
te amo.

Poesía Durangoa

A spontaneous poem that came out of me as if by itself when hiking in the beautiful mountains above Durango, Basque Country

The float

In this absolute moment, a pen is held by a hand, writing what the camera of a mobile phone can't capture.

Thoughts and ideas swirl away, let to rest on the mountainside, replaced by an unspeakable frisson. At peace with the self, and that unvisible viceroy, floating with the current of the whirlpool, that change rhythm and calms to a rill, while the happy soul floats along in its comforting puddles. In this absolute moment.

Secret spot somewhere in Euskadi

Where ivy is
allowed to
grow

Embosomed window frames, leaves that filter, saving the home from what's outside; frenzy, evil predators, smoke.

The ivy grows happily, it does not hear, does not see. It only feels its way upward, along small, tiny ledges, cracks in the facade, imperfections.

There! Halfway up, some branches go their own way, testing new ideas. The ivy does not shy away for the doing of its extremities, it is the imperative.

The self-righteous animals call it ignorance, but it doesn't listen. Now, see, it tries again! It dares to make mistakes, discovers new things. Live.

We can listen but don't. Maybe there, behind the ivy, that we dare.

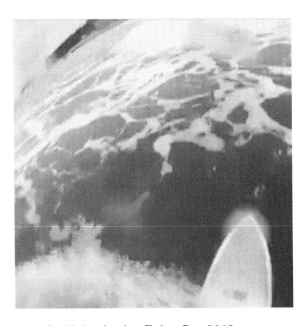

Torö, Stockholm, Sweden. Fathers Day 2013

I bow before you

Nine years ago, the ocean was my refuge. It was surfing I survived on then.

The marriage lay in ruins, my sensory organs wounded and bleeding in attempts to understand. My throbbing head only produced concerns about what would happen to my daughters if we broke up, when we broke up. It was a fact that I couldn't resist for much longer.

This was nine years ago. All these difficult years are now behind me. New obstacles will appear on my enlightened path, but surfing, the sea, and the minimalist life in my rolling home took me out of my crisis, and will do so again and again. This choice of existence created a strong and happy father of the loser I almost lost myself to. And whatever happens, the sea will continue to roll its life giving force over the steel-blue planet long after I have turned back into water. I'm already one with it.

Thank you big blue.

Immortal for a moment

Cogito ergo sum – I think therefore I am. To have a book about my life read by others, do I exist more then? When the dust has settled in between every page, am I not then gone forever? Do I rise from the dead when my thoughts and deeds are heard pronounced again? Am I let to be for an exquisite moment?

Imagine being immortal, just the thought when it's thought.

New Year 2020/21

What if there is no new year? Time might only be a fictional concept, a human invention trying to make a continuous flow, with neither start nor finish, understandable.

What if we saw life when it happened more vividly than remembering it or dreaming about it? What if we stopped counting and comparing?

The power of acrylic fizz

A not so cool place transformed into something interesting, almost beautiful. Graffiti can be a nuisance, a sabotage, tags for the sake of egoistic minds, – Look at me, I am someone! But rightly done it can tear fear and sadness into molecules and create food for new thoughts.

The abandoned military base in Parede, Lisbon

Limbo-land

I'm a slow starter, I work best that way. Letting my conscious-ness switch from the parallel dream world into the real at its own pace. Hovering between these two states, inside my blue survival capsule, writing is at its most surreal, strangely also at its most tangible, when daytime dreams get down to the exact words. This is the no-man's-land where I find my truth.

Reading out loud is good practice, hearing the sound, feeling its vibration on lips and tongue, noticing what it does to my surroundings. Today some snails gathered around in small groups and pairs, as if consoled by the sound of my thoughts. They sat themselves down in hearing distance, on the leaves of a bush outside my door, curled inside their shells in a trance like state. I saw a couple holding hands. What do I know, I'm in the Limbo-land.

Pelota Basque

The sound of crushing hand-bones, swollen and muscular
to abnormal proportions, they swing and swing. The pain
they endure to stand a full game, smiling at it, a ritual of
endurance and elegance with us spectators in awe.

Life : II

There are different ways of looking at life, you choose what fits you best. I've set out to see the beauty before what's broken or wrong.

The undead dandy

A product of his time, there he sat in the last, curved rays of
a set sun. A prey obeying codes of beasts.

Caption to my friend Robin Falxa's painting
Visit his Instagram for the full colour version

Sare, Iparralde, Pais Basque

A word by a decaying house

Structures and patterns, the fibres of life coming to the surface. Ageing or maturing, enduring or enjoying. The different phases, the unexpected twists and turns, it's up to you to make it anything but a slow wait for death.

Cannibalism.
With the right set of eyes, or wrong.

This place has problems getting tourists, or just anyone obeying road signs.

Encounters of a life time

I found a beach where a foxy sand lady reigned. Then I saw
her disappear, never to seduce again.

São Juliâo, Ericeira

And what about the petrified Basque warrior who told me the story and the whereabouts of the Holy Grail.

Two of nature's many works of art

Survivors and deadbeats

The hidden worlds, distinguishing man from men. Considering it a no-go or a must-do was earlier a question of survival. What are we now, will we survive?

Cave in the forest above Sare, in line with the directions of the Basque warrior. Is this where the Cathars hid the sacred goblet?

Coincidence, sign or warning

The curtains, installed in my Beatrice in the bleak autumn of 2018… Doesn't the pattern resemble something familiar that happened one and a half years later?

#covid

Quarantine paranoia,
or lively imagination

Look at that rock in the background, look at its ribbed, elephant skin. Blue shadows in the grey, depressions in the rocky wall, hollowed out by erosion and earthquake. At its foot, the edgy masses that once collapsed with roaring screams, then comforted by wet and salt. The outcast hard and heavy slowly purified into fine-grained happiness.

The sand now flows with the tidal currents. Sometimes though, it looks up to its origin and thinks of life and its unfathomable mess. Up there, the pride and security lay in looking down on others. Up there it saw no better existence. But time did not end when the rock cracked, it had been a misconception. The below gifted joy, had a sea that healed, gave movement and life to what had been rigid and locked into a fix.

In front of the elephant, another cliff with another story. Gaping in surprise, half the body torn off at the crown of its green meadow.

Once a rolling hill, mimicking the swell of the sea out there, the friendly expression it has before crashing onto shore, twisting its froth and making thunder, and shaking the ground.

For oceans of time it endured all anxious elements, and the beating of its feet. Then one day the giant had to give up, it still came as a surprise.

"Why so much of me? Why me at all?"

Until this day it shouts and cries towards the horizon. The screaming rock regrets its fate every day the shadows open its gaping mouth. And aren't the surroundings looking at it, compassionate but also in shame? One cannot question the course of life and the ruler of time.

There it stands, the leper rock non grata, wishing it soon collapsed and allowed to vanish. Forgetting about the fine-grained joy, and all the sunny days to come.

During Portugal's first lockdown, I stood just north of Sagres, staring southwards, day after day.

41

A story from a time we
soon have forgotten

A man is standing silently outside his dented, blue camper-van. He has no other option than to be patient, confined to solitude for almost two months. The picture doesn't disclose his fortunate location in south Portugal, far from the harsh restrictions put upon city dwellers in central Europe and around the world. No, despite the pure luck of being at the right place at a very wrong time in history, this man longed for a special activity that had been made illegal. He was about to burst out and cry, as the human child he really was. What an egoistic thought it was. Then news came on the little device; it was said that the coming week would see the start back to normality, with the lifting of restrictions most importantly. He was crossing his fingers so hard he could hear the joints crack, hoping that he finally would be allowed to surf.

He drank some red wine, took this picture, and wrote a short story about a time we soon have forgotten.

Life : III

Life goes on, it always does. Continuing, evolving, unpredict-
able is its path, but on it goes. Nothing stops it, that you can
trust. Don't feel stress or fear, float with the stream that is life,
don't fight against the current. The next sunrise awaits.

Rice-Otto

Otto made rice every day for many, many years. He got
bored with it, it was dull. People even made fun of him,
"Look, here comes Rice-Otto!" They laughed, Otto cried.
Salty tears ran down the rice, mushrooms fell down in it as
well (I don't know how but they did), in his bitterness he
tore lemons into it just to make it worse. It turned out to be
a delicious dish, so delicious that he soon went on to be the
most popular guy in the village. He later used this mascu-
line popularity in the local red-light district, that was big at
that time, and sadly succumbed to drugs only a decade later.
But that's another story. I just wanted to tell you how the
name of this dish came to be.

#historylesson #notreally
#humor #queastionable

The setting sun

It has pointed towards us for eternity, the hand stretched out, and a finger eager to be touched.

It has looked directly into the eyes of every man, woman and creature with the calming message of happiness and respect.

It has sent us tranquillity beam by beam, only wishing we would touch it back some day.

At dawn humans listened to this wisdom and fingertipped the sorce as it was meant, as animals still do.

But what happened then? How could greed shine brighter than this? "Gold!" Screams the civilized with unquenched thirst, forgetting it's a mere copy that melts and twists in agony as we push onwards, towards death.

#rainbowwarriors

Funny story, for you...

I had a quick look at the weather app and decided to take the board inside. Tomorrow, early morning, Beatrice is going to the mechanics. And as she is to sleep over a night or two I don't want to keep my precious Andreini on the roof. The app warned it would rain furry animals during the night, so I figured it better not to wait bringing her in. It was a smart move, doing it in the dry...

Beatrice's wooden interior has been kept in good condition because of one rule; never ever bring anything wet inside.

After a lot of hustle, involving the strapping to the ceiling inside my tiny camper, I felt worthy of a good night's sleep. Then suddenly, a rather big amount of water that appeard trapped inside the boardbag started to leak out, dripping down on me like a malfunctioning sprinkler. It was not fun and several words from the hidden pages of both Swedish, Spanish and English dictionaries were uttered, loudly.

Now finaly the indoor rain has stopped but I am too tired to change the bed linen. A quick look at the weather app again; it seems it won't rain after all...

Good night.

Nature touches me

Here I stand
Swept in coasts of heaving waters
A sun filters through cloudy skies
Stillness before a storm

Is our world only a tiny ball in infinite space?

As I turn around
the sun breaks free
the water forms a perfect wave
hugging the sandy shores

It tries to tell me something

We are humans
we are the most evil creatures ever lived
consuming all and demanding more
How can we not see that nature has had enough?

"Help me!" it cries

A ripple bounces off a rock and disappears out to sea

All these poor humans

There are many who yearn to be president, or perhaps CEO, if possible appointed King. That's what one should be, that's what one should strive for, it is the meaning of life. This is how many go by their day. But, those who work hard to reach this goal of theirs, and fight, for power, money and honour, gods or political doctrines, all day, all the time. Are they living? Is not real happiness given those who dare to stop and breathe?

Imagine if we set our aim differently; if we rejoiced the moment, in the moment, without giving a thought on new or more, without demanding others to follow but welcoming them one by one.

Imagine life like that.

To my daughter

The epileptic kaleidoscope

Are all diseases curses, or are they gifts of god? We are at least free to look at them as we please, so why not a cosmos attempt to give us shortsighted humans a glimmer of the primordial power. Too great to be given as a whole, it comes to us clothed in pain, suffering and alienation. Only then we listen to lightning and thunder that in milliseconds link new thoughts and logics, which we, the herd-animal, miss in our fear of the inconsistent.

My sweet, beautiful daughter. I want to comfort you in your cries over the "disease", as you call it, lips quivering.

"Will I always have it, Dad?"

My childhood memories are also rags and patchwork. Large gaps filled with chimeras and rationalizations in an effort to understand my own existence. But just like you, who amaze your surroundings with insightful thoughts and comments from time to time, here and there amongst my black holes are razor-sharp sequences that take me back in time and space with an absolute pitch.

My childhood epilepsy effaced much of my time and my thinking. It also was as if my epilepsy sometimes allowed the synapses to be connected to the last connection, letting radiant light penetrate all the black with wonderful and clear logical explanations to observations and questions. It came to me in a way it didn't seem to do for others.

A memory, one of those razor-sharp. I was five years old and stood between my parents and an angry farmer, interrupting their dispute over the docking of our boat. My words made them drop their chins and arms. "Well, you're right I suppose." Said the farmer, and my parents looked just as ashamed. We walked quietly to our boat and the farmer in opposite direction, I with my inner strength on the surface for a short moment. The one I knew I possessed but rarely was allowed to show. The one I wanted everyone to see, rather then the half-witted idiot I came to be cast as. Having difficulties with memory and dyslexia, I was a lazy boy with low capacity, all while complex thoughts I couldn't dress in words or deeds seethed on my inside. My mocked head sunk into the shoulders, convinced they were right, with the little brightness in me suffocated and silenced.

I won't let this sad history happen to you my love. Listen to what I have to say.

In some way this self depraving disillusion continued until current days. I grew out of the seizures and the measurable epilepsy, but I'm still unable to control my bright moments and have been ashamed of my short-comings that are just as impossible to predict. Until the day I decided to break free. Then I understood what was, actually, my little greatness.

Let me explain.

Imagine a kaleidoscope, but instead of flakes of colours, there are holes in the multi layer discs that rotate and interact. When the holes of the discs align, then light is let in. In my kaleidoscope, the discs are many and the holes are of different shapes and sizes. It takes years for a full lap, or perhaps only a few hours, and I can't control the rotation. Long time can pass between the lights shining through, but here and there glimpses of the great truth is presented to me. In that flash of a moment I try to write or be creative. From the outside it might appear hyperactive or manic, but I only try to savour the light before it goes out again. Just like these words and sentences that were written down after the morning coffee, sitting at the foot of the Nazaré lighthouse. Yes, the one with the biggest waves in the world hitting the shores below.

Today the ocean is flat, and I'm the exact opposite for a while, and without the fear of being devalued by others.

This is the key for you and me, my dear daughter. Try to ignore the demands of others and your desire to show yourself of value. Try to feel confidence in what you are, keep your head high above your splendid shoulders. You have your little greatness in you, be proud of it. Your audience simply has to wait until your kaleidoscope aligns.

I see the light in you. You radiate strongly and clearly before the darkness recedes. You do it more often and more illuminated than I did. Rest assured, one day you will see what I see, and further beyond the horizon. Hang on to your magic viewing glass and believe in yourself.

Praia Gigi, Baleal. 9´0 Gato Heroi Glider-Gun.
Photo: Daniel Espírito Santo.

Beatrice at the foot of Sintra

My choice

My Beatrice, you were the best or perhaps the only solution to the situation I was in, but you turned out to be much more than that.

I love you dearly, as a companion more than a vehicle, your rugged exterior and cosy interior. You've taken me on adventures around Southern Europe, to surf-spots, ski-slopes, beautiful landscapes and picturesque villages, letting me meet genuine people on the way. All the funny and eye-opening coincidences that I have been treated to are all thanks to you, my tiny mobile home since four years.

Last night we slept through one of many cold nights, but we've had worse and now it's part of our cleanse, the epicurean way – enjoying every minute, trying to look positive on everything that happens and accept the way our life continues on our path.

I'm far from perfect, but Beatrice is leading the way and I feel very happy that she does.

#campervan #epicureanism #lessismore
#minimalism

The percolator's view on life

I've used it everyday for several years. I always do it the same way, the same amount of water and coffee powder. But somehow there are very big differences in how much coffee it produces. One morning it's a full cup, the next day only half a cup. Today it fizzes gently, other days it boils over the rim. It varies greatly.

Temperature and pressure of the air around it, other minute factors play also a role. How compact the powder is packed, the powder itself, the coffee manufacturers wrong or right doings. I can't affect the size of the grain, nor the weather where I sit. I have to take it as it comes, just like I should do with life.

#life #acceptance

Night sky over Beatrice

The Sintra forest

A transparent mirror

Not reflecting, undressing
teared off, naked

Skin of milky glass

Beams of colours
filtering down
into hues of grey
An ash of what really is

The true believer

I have holes in my hands
There are holes in my hands
Can you see the holes in my hands?
Here are the holes in my hands
You see them
You feel them

But there are no holes in my hands
I pushed you

Incalculable

To read is not to count the words. Writing is not setting up equations. A story cannot be calculated or predicted, it must be felt. It is not possible to point your finger to a map and say, "Here is the good story!" The same goes for the time it was written. What was cheered on yesterday can be booed at tomorrow, and with that comes the realization that a boo can be a hooray the very next day again. It is not possible to be sure about the future, it is even more difficult to decide what is good or bad, right or wrong, correct or forbidden, over the heads of others.

A good story is usually written on thoughts that are not yours, not even thought as you think. A thought that tease your emotional whiskers, preferably against the grain, justifies its existence. This is where real reading is had, on paths you have never walked, with characters you have never met, and events you never have been able to imagine in the windowless room. To empathize instead of criticize or judge, is the only way to behold a good story.

So why do we still choose the same black hole of un-imaginative stories all too often. Psychopathic murderers in the bookshelves and Marvel heroes streamed into every device. Why? We already know how it ends.

Unfortunately, this is also the case with the currents of opinions and conceptions. It is easy to fall into the ranks of the right or the left; liberals, moderates, socialists, feminists, racists, fascists, and the selfish elitists calling themselves pluralists.

Doctrines have clear frameworks and are easier to live by, right and wrong are black and white. As our society has become more and more complex and complicated, our positions on any issue are simplified as our brains burn their last fuse. All the musts and demands, of career and material prosperity; go to the gym, be a parent and partner and a reliable employee, and a woke and correct, for and against, righteous human by all means.

Already a long time ago, we stopped and shut down, stuck our heads in the ground. Ignoring the danger of ignorance. And this state of mind is not going to make a good story, or history if we choose to call it so.

Over our heads the ruling masters loudly roar. Men and women, all convinced that it is their time now. All or nothing, make or break, with the index finger on the button of doom. And the little man just behind, who has found his place and blindly obeys, ignoring human reflexes in fear of falling behind. It's their time too, and everyone after them in the same way. No one steps aside, no one dare to listen or feel. They do not have the courage left, we do not have the courage left. No one wants to make a mistake at this point. We calculate and compute, it's easier. Tapping the keyboard and distance ourselves from reality.

But what if we didn't hate each other so easily? What if we accepted differences, seeing flaws and errors as attempts to find new rights? What if we stopped trolling after only reading the first paragraph? What if we listened and felt? What if the Russians, the Americans, the Chinese, the religious fundamentalists and the economic interests created nations they themselves would like to live in, instead of putting all the money and gods on Dubai and Monaco? What if the headlines wrote peace?

"I have a dream"

In my dream the media and the politicians don't write a word about the person or persona behind conflicting arguments, instead they put all their intellectual power on presenting their answer without patronizing or censorship. In the dream there are no fixed doctrines, and no intriguing is done to seize power. The only thing existing are different worldviews and their arguments, and the insight that one sometimes wins over the other, accepting that the power isn't always in the same hands.

In this dream, everyone is happily humble, repairing what is broken. In this dream those who have don't grasp for more before lending a helping hand. Love is plentiful, and hate is a four-letter word children are taught to avoid in school.

Close your eyes and try to see it.

Now is more than then

Here I step through the history of my own life. Well, you might say; it won't be history until later. My friend, weren't the experiences you now remember with joy even more valuable when you had them? Seeing what will become before it is done and over, wouldn't that make you settle with existence?

Horizons

If a bluff, a small mountain, or even the crown of a tall forest in the near distance, has been the furthest you've been let to see. That would be your horizon then. What if you climbed the hill or the tallest tree, would that change your beliefs? Would you see the real horizon then? This line far away is always somewhere else and unreachable, but often thought of as if a fixed point, promising advantages and profits beyond your standing ground. A contraption I tell you, don't build your existence on it.

Persona without a person

In the past a persona was an expression of a character with a strong idea. Now the idea is increasingly invisible. Left are only nice faces and fashionable clothes, amazing and impressing us as long as it sticks to the program. An Andy Warhol wonderland, copies of copies en masse, where no-one ever tries anything new, never risk doing wrong outside affixed templates. Here we soon speak without words, here we soon live the aftermaths.

Thoughts we have when we talk

We are locked in a world of internal conflicts. Everything outside is a reaction to what's within; like when we shout, when we judge, and when we attack to defend. Whatever monsters we think we fight, it is nothing but an antagonist projected by the evil parasite.

Yourself

I'm a hobo, I'm a drunk, I'm a vagrant dissident. I might be that in your eyes. What you don't see is that I'm not at the far end of you. I am in the middle. And the gravity of up and down does not apply; it's merely a slide along a horizontal plane.

And the war began

A vegetable named Pickles was ridiculed by a cucumber in vinegar, in a jar on a shelf on the other side of the aisle.

Constrained to abnormality

Why is it that archaeologists only find ancient remains in square and geometric shapes, contrary to nature's organic pretzel hooks? The learned professors constrain their admiration of forgotten civilizations to findings differing from how nature would have done it, and its original gardeners.

Derail

Here I walk on a road by the sea. Next to me a railway, straight and rigid, where trains hurry to reach their destiny, where the living second is a needle sting, and where blunt stops empty their guts at the very end.

Here I walk on a road by the sea, with my legs and feet, on gravel and roots, allowed to feel, to touch, to ask the questions. Here I walk, far from my intended iron lane.

Railroad crossing, Cenitz, Pays Basque

Before the lock-down.
Foz do Lizandro, Ericeira

Crocodile

Dreaming back, no I shouldn't I say
See you later crocodile

Before there was green grass,
now barren, plagued and brown
Give up the thoughts of a blue balloon,
it would burst and drown. Let it fly
No one can change the direction of time
See you later crocodile

I'm lost and out of play I say
No, look here my friend, it is not fully so
Let's taste this grey and fly still again,
a flight of another sort, a new hurray
See you soon crocodile

Goodbye, for now

The last couple of years have been a great trip. I got further than I've ever been. I grew as a human by learning how to flow with the rhythm of life, trusting my self and energies around me.

Now starts a new journey. What will happen? What great personalities will I meet this time? What unique life altering coincidences will I experience in my little campervan called Beatrice? The only thing certain is that it is going to be a true tale lived and told here and now, well off the beaten path.

See you there!

Coming novels

My time in the sun (English - October 2022)
This is actually the prologue to my debut novel, diary, and travelogue in one – The Swede who let go – but preferably read after. This is the story about how I came to live in Dominican Republic for twelve years, and all the marvels and cultural clashes that came with it.

The love of a surfboard (English – November 2022)
Many of us have had one board that stood out from the rest, the magic one. All of us have heard stories about them, here's the tale about mine.

Det osynliga (Svenska – December 2022)
Fiction. En spegelvärld där ytterligheter dominerar. Ena stunden för, sedan emot, alltid lika övertygad om sin egen sidas rätt över den andres. Hur kan de inte se balansen där emellan? Vem bär skulden, vad är drivkraften, vem vinner slaget?

Printed by Amazon Italia Logistica S.r.l.
Torrazza Piemonte (TO), Italy

36220058R00048